This book belongs to:

· ·

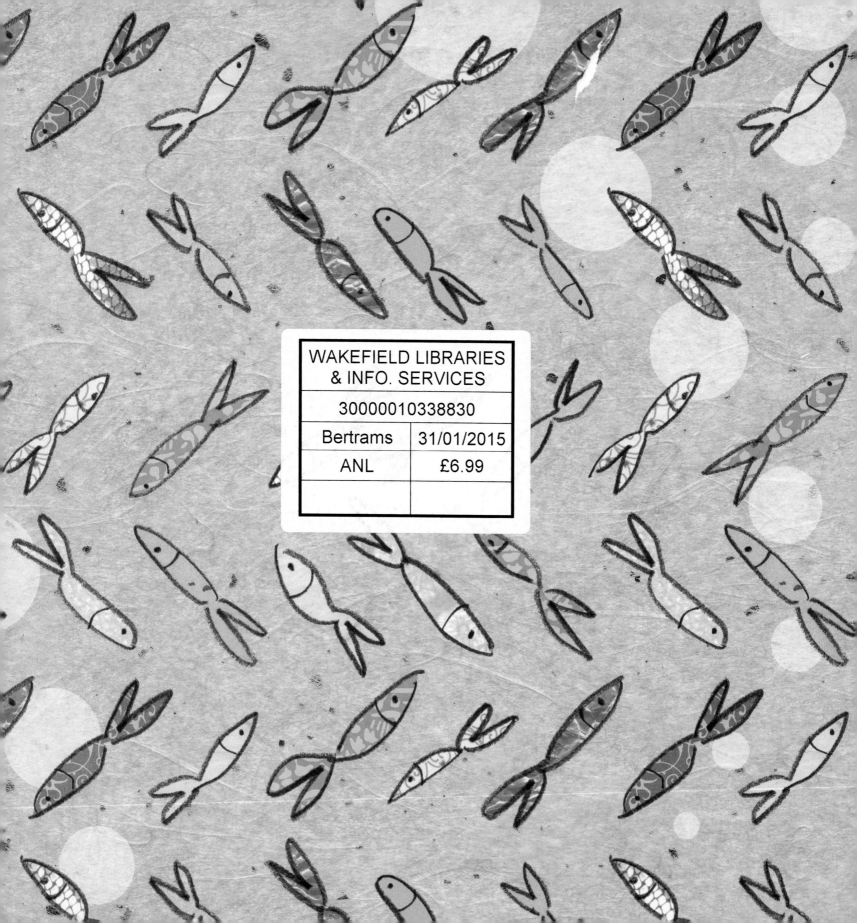

Rebecca Ashdown

Bob AND Flo

the missing bucket

OXFORD

UNIVERSITY PRESS

It was Flo's first day at nursery.

She had a packed lunch and a new bow.

'I like your bow,' said a little penguin.
'I like your bucket,' said another.
His name was Bob.

'Thanks,' said Flo.

Flo tried some painting.

But then she noticed her
bucket was missing . . .

and there

was something slightly different about

Bob.

So Flo
went
to look
for her
bucket.

Bob was playing with the bricks.

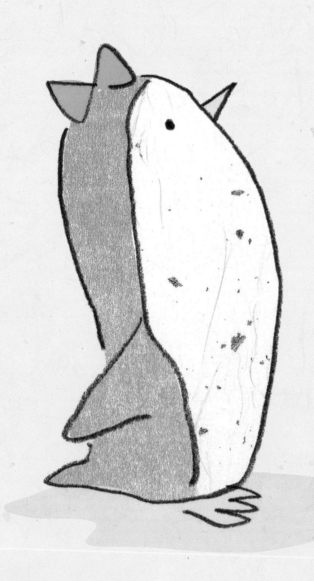

'I like
your
tower,'
said Flo.

'Thanks,'
said Bob.

There were some lovely
sandcastles outside.

But where was Flo's

bucket?

After lunch,

Flo went to play on the slide . . .

and **there** was her bucket!

But where was Bob?

Stuck!

Flo had an idea.

WHOOSH

went the water.

'Thanks!'
said Bob.

WHOOSH

WHOOSH

all afternoon until it was time to go home.

'Bye bye,'
giggled
Bob.

'See you tomorrow,' said Flo.
'And don't forget **our bucket!**'

For Tate and Rufus

OXFORD
UNIVERSITY PRESS

Great Clarendon Street, Oxford OX2 6DP

Oxford University Press is a department of the University of Oxford.
It furthers the University's objective of excellence in research, scholarship,
and education by publishing worldwide in

Oxford New York

Auckland Cape Town Dar es Salaam Hong Kong Karachi
Kuala Lumpur Madrid Melbourne Mexico City Nairobi
New Delhi Shanghai Taipei Toronto

With offices in
Argentina Austria Brazil Chile Czech Republic France Greece
Guatemala Hungary Italy Japan Poland Portugal Singapore
South Korea Switzerland Thailand Turkey Ukraine Vietnam

Text and illustrations copyright © Rebecca Ashdown 2014
The moral rights of the author and artist have been asserted

Database right Oxford University Press (maker)

First published 2014

First published in paperback 2015

British Library Cataloguing in Publication Data available

ISBN: 978-0-19-273713-7 (paperback)

2 4 6 8 10 9 7 5 3 1

Printed in China

Paper used in the production of this book is a natural, recyclable product made
from wood grown in sustainable forests. The manufacturing process conforms
to the environmental regulations of the country of origin

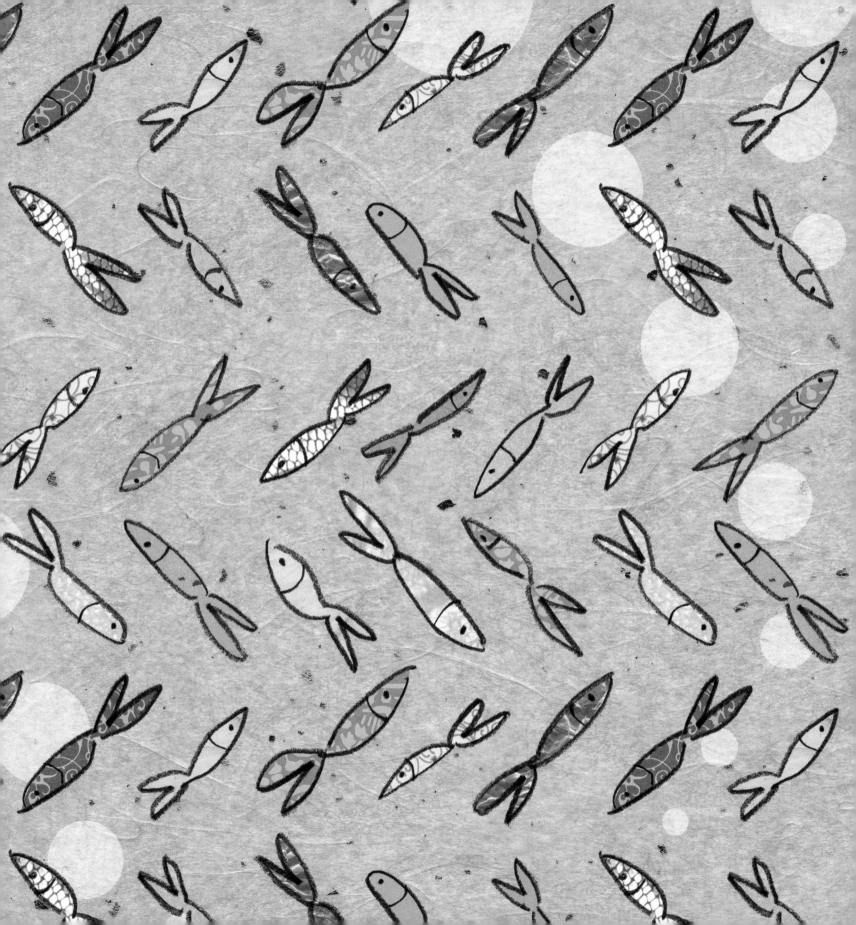